An Incredible Journey Book

Knights in New York

Book
Six

by Connie Lee Berry

A super big hello to Sydney's best friend Marc, her friend Luca, and to friends in her class: Bianca, Kaylee, Cameron, Jesse, Austin, Jack, Warren, Anna, Amanda, Katie, Kaitlyn, Rahul, Schuyler, Jack A., Gaige, and Gianna. Thanks for a great year to Mrs. Krueger, Mrs. Gault, and Mrs. Acosta. Thanks to Mrs. Hawley's class for making this book part of their class project.

This book is dedicated to my two big boys who journeyed to New York with me in freezing weather to check out the city. Thank you.

ISBN-13: 978-0977284856

TABLE OF CONTENTS

Cool Facts About New York City

New York City is the most populous city in the U.S.A. It consists of five boroughs: The Bronx, Brooklyn, Manhattan, Queens, and Staten Island.

New York City has 722 miles of subway track.

The *New York Post,* established in 1801 by Alexander Hamilton, is the oldest daily running newspaper in the United States.

The first capital of the United States was New York City. In 1789, George Washington took his oath as president on the balcony of Federal Hall.

Gennaro Lombardi opened the first United States pizzeria in 1905 in New York City.

The Big Apple is the nickname for New York City made popular by John J. Fitzgerald, a sports writer, who wrote a column called "Around the Big Apple." The writer said he first heard the term used by stable hands in New Orleans, who referred to New York's racetracks as the Big Apple, or the ultimate goal.

New York Landmark Riddles

(Don't forget to cover up the answers at the bottom.)

1. Architect Frank Lloyd Wright died before this
   building of modern art was done.
   To look at its spiral design is so much fun!

2. It's a museum where dinosaur bones can be found.
   It's one of the best natural science displays around.

3. This city arena bears a famous name.
   Concerts and sporting events are its claim to fame.

4. This seventy-seven-story skyscraper was the
   tallest building in the world for a year.
   The top of it has steel arches, triangular windows,
   and automotive gear.

5. Splendid music can be heard coming from this
   1891 great hall. Its stage has seen composers,
   opera singers, and musicians—the most famous
   of them all.

1. Guggenheim Museum 2. American Museum of Natural History
3. Madison Square Garden 4. Chrysler Building 5. Carnegie Hall

Prologue

In the first Incredible Journey Book, *The Criminal in the Caymans*, two mysterious boxes arrived on Max and Sam's doorstep. In one box, they found an old leather journal. Inside the journal was yellowed paper with a note scribbled on the first page that said, "Notes taken wisely can be of great use to you." In the second box, they found a map dated October 11, 1964 and labeled "Max and Sam's Incredible Journey Map."

Since that time, a new letter has mysteriously appeared on the map with each trip they take. In the Cayman Islands, a "W" appeared . . . in Tahiti, an "I" . . . in Africa, an "S" . . . in the Virgin Islands, a "D" . . . and in Mexico, an "O" appeared.

Max and Sam have not discovered who sent the map or the journal or why the letters keep appearing on the map. One of these mysteries will be solved in this book. The other will be solved in a later book.

ONE

EMBARRASSING STICKERS

The bright sun beamed down on the Stone family's van as it moved slowly down the highway. The temperature reading on the dashboard said it was already ninety degrees outside. Even the palm trees lining the freeway seemed to be wilting in the morning's blistering heat. If it wasn't for the daily afternoon rain shower to rescue the vegetation from the brutality of the sun, Florida would look like a desert by now.

Mrs. Stone wiped her sweaty forehead

with a tissue. The air conditioning in the vehicle still hadn't cooled her down from the hectic morning of rushing around, trying to find clothing to pack for the boys' three-day trip. After all, they had just gotten back from Mexico the night before.

The Stone family had stayed an extra day in Mexico to find out what the archeologist's findings were. Their heads were still spinning with excitement about the amazing discovery they had made—an ancient mummy along with its precious artifacts—all verified to be genuine by Dr. Martin, a renowned specialist in his field.

"Oh, no!" Mrs. Stone yelled, looking at her husband. "Did I pack their jackets?"

"We won't need jackets in *July*," Sam said from the van's second row, looking up at his mom like she had lost her marbles.

"You might," she answered back. "It gets chilly at night sometimes. . . . Besides, it rains a lot there in the summer."

"We'll survive," Max mumbled.

In a split second, Mrs. Stone moved on to another worry. "Why is the traffic so crazy here? We're just creeping along when you have a flight to catch. Why can't our city have a subway like New York?"

"New York is much bigger than Tampa for one thing," Sam said. "Besides the subway system seems confusing with all the different trains going everywhere."

"You might have a hard time getting around the city," Mrs. Stone said, frowning with the realization. "I don't think your aunt has ridden on a subway before."

Sam groaned.

"We'll figure it out," Max said. "We'll ask for directions if we get lost."

The traffic picked up all of a sudden, and they cringed as they passed a wrecker pulling a smashed car.

"I bet *that's* the culprit of our delay," Mr. Stone said quietly. "I hope no one got hurt." He sighed.

Mrs. Stone switched to a more cheerful subject. "You're going to have so much fun on your trip," she gushed. "Are you scared to fly alone?"

"We've flown so many times lately, it'll be easy," Sam said, looking out the window toward the sky to watch an airplane that had just taken off. He realized they were near the airport.

"Don't forget to wait by the gate for your aunt," Mrs. Stone reminded them. "Her flight from Kentucky connects through Memphis and gets in a few minutes before yours. The airline won't release you until she gets there."

"We don't even know what she looks like," Max said.

"Don't worry," their mom assured them. "I sent her a recent photo of you, so she'll find *you*. Besides, you saw your cousin Madison in Africa, so you'll recognize her.

She is staying with your aunt for the rest of the summer while her parents are in England. The company her dad works for sent him overseas for a couple of months to train workers there. You were just two and three the last time your aunt saw you. How time flies. . . ."

Mrs. Stone was in her own world of thought when Sam asked a question. "Are you going somewhere to watch the fireworks tonight?" he said, suddenly remembering that it was the Fourth of July.

Their mom continued to reminisce. "The last time you saw your aunt was when we went to Kentucky for your grandma's seventieth birthday party. You guys were so cute then."

"Don't start that stuff again," Max pleaded. "We're not going away for good."

"We're taking Sydney to a park tonight to watch fireworks," Mr. Stone said, answering Sam's question as he drove the van through the busy airport complex and followed the signs to the departure drop-off area.

"You're staying at a hotel near Central Park tonight," their mom informed them. "Your aunt said the hotel sounds nice."

Mr. Stone pulled the van over to the curb and went to the back of the van to open the trunk. While he carried his sons' suitcases over to the outdoor check-in counter, Mrs. Stone and the boys made their way out of the van. Mrs. Stone rummaged through her cluttered purse, still filled with brochures and receipts from Mexico, to find the tickets.

"Whew!" she finally said. "I was beginning to think I left these at home."

She handed the tickets to a tall bald man behind the counter and smiled, content that they had managed to make it to the airport in time.

The boys followed her lead and relaxed

for a moment. It was a relief that the roof above them protected their skin from the pounding sun, even though the air around them smelled musty. The boys stared at the tags the man had wrapped around the handles of their luggage.

Sam noticed the letters "LGA" and nudged his mom to see if she knew what they stood for.

"The letters stand for Laguardia Airport

in New York," she said. "That's the airport you'll be flying into."

"How many airports are there in New York?" Sam asked.

"Let's see," their mom said, thinking. "There's Laguardia—and JFK—I guess there's three major airports if you count the one in Newark, New Jersey."

The tall man handed Mrs. Stone a packet. "The boys' boarding passes and unaccompanied minor documentation is inside along with their return tickets to Tampa," he said. "I've printed you a pass to get through the security checkpoint so that you can walk the boys to the gate. Have a good morning."

Mr. Stone turned to his sons, who already had their carry-on bags over their shoulders. "You're going to do just fine," he said, hugging them. "Stay far away from trouble," he warned. "I'll drive the van around and wait for you at the baggage claim curb," he said to his wife.

As Mrs. Stone, Max, and Sam made their way through the doors . . . up the escalator . . . onto the tram . . . and through the security checkpoint, Max and Sam looked around at the abstract, colorful art that splashed out from the shiny chrome walls. This airport looked modern compared to the smaller tropical ones they had traveled through in Mexico and the Caribbean. Even though this space was large and industrial-looking, the airport's bold-patterned carpet and artwork made the place cheerful and inviting.

After the Stone family had walked to the gate, Max and Sam waited in line for their turn to go down the jetway to the plane. They groaned when a ticket agent scanned the bar codes of their tickets and slapped big white stickers on their chests that displayed the words "Unaccompanied Minor" in bold red letters.

"We're marked!" Sam said, chuckling. "And to think that I thought we might get away with posing as adults for a day."

A thought struck their mom. "Oh no, you don't," she said eyeing them furiously. "Don't take those stickers off—embarrassing or not."

Max and Sam grinned teasingly at their mom one last time before heading down the jetway.

Mrs. Stone felt like a nervous mother sending her kids off to kindergarten on the first day. She fidgeted and shouted words of wisdom until they were out of sight. "Behave," she called out to them. "Be careful—it's a big city—call me."

I must be *crazy* sending the two of them to a big city, she thought. The boys found a way to get into messes in even the smallest of places—in the middle of nowhere, in fact. What turmoil would they get themselves into in a place like New York?

FLIGHT TO NEW YORK

The boys were escorted to their seats by a flight attendant who humiliated them even further by giving them a private briefing on the emergency exits.

After an announcement that the aircraft door would soon be closing, the boys settled in for a three-hour flight. Sam took out a comic book from his bag and scooted over to the window seat, leaving the center seat empty between him and his brother.

Max switched on his overhead reading light and took out a book about New York.

He leaned over to his brother. "I have a feeling you're not going to be much help in New York. I've been studying this book for hours, and I haven't seen you look at it once. I guess I'll carry us like always."

"*What*?" Sam yelled out. "Are you serious?"

"Are you boys okay?" a voice interrupted.

The boys blushed when they looked up to see a flight attendant standing over them. "It doesn't solve anything when you fight," she lectured. "Can't you boys be civil to each other, at least for the flight?"

"Yes, ma'am," Sam said shyly, thinking that the lady must be a mom herself. She seemed comfortable giving children advice.

"And how about you?" the lady said, staring at Max, waiting for an answer.

"Yes, ma'am," he said quickly before glancing down at his book.

Max's face burned with embarrassment for a few moments before he recovered enough to open his book. He was eager to learn about Central Park. He read:

Central Park, an 843-acre nature oasis in Manhattan in New York City filled with beautiful lakes, ponds, and meadows, was created by planting thousands of trees and plants. The park has over twenty-five million visitors a year, making it the most visited city park in the United States. There are many attractions located within the park such as walking and running tracks, ice-skating rinks for the winter, a zoo, an outdoor theater, a nature center in Belvedere Castle, a historic carousel, carriage-horse rides, playgrounds for children, and grass areas for team sports and concerts.

After studying his book for a while, Max remembered the Renaissance Festival brochure they had received in the mail. He eagerly reached down and found it in his bag. Touching it made him fill with anticipation. He read it word for word.

New York is honored to host a medieval festival in Central Park on the Great Lawn this year. On the venue will be a jousting competition at eleven o'clock, followed by a feast fit for a king. At two o'clock, nonresidents of New York can test their knowledge of the city's landmarks by competing in the Knights of Knowledge contest.

Max closed the brochure and drifted off to sleep. He woke up a couple of hours later from the sound of a bell. An announcement followed that said:

We are now beginning our descent into New York's Laguardia Airport. Please stow any luggage you may have gotten out during the flight. It is a beautiful morning in New York City, sunny and eighty-five degrees Fahrenheit. We'll be at the gate at 11:30. New York is in the eastern time zone. It has been our pleasure having you on today's flight.

THREE

THE WEATHER PROBLEM

When the plane came to a standstill at the gate, Max and Sam waited in their seats while everyone deplaned, just as they had been instructed to do. They waited patiently as the attendant gathered up her belongings so she could walk them to the gate area.

"Just one more thing," she said, running back to her jump seat for a bottle of water.

Her southern drawl gave away the fact that she was not from New York. "Come on, y'all," she said to them as she passed their seats, her luggage rolling behind her. "I'm excited about being here."

The boys slid out of their row of seats and followed her down the narrow aisle of the plane and down the jetway, letting their bags hang off of their shoulders.

When they got to the gate area, she stopped to open their ticket packet. "Oh, there it is," she said, studying the top document. "You're meeting your aunt here?"

"Yes," Sam answered. "She just came in from another flight. She may not be here yet."

"Where did her flight come from? I'll check to see if it's arrived," the attendant said.

"A flight from Kentucky," Sam said. "I think she had to go through Memphis."

"Uh-oh," the lady mumbled under her breath. "Not a good sign."

Max and Sam stared at her, trying to figure out what she meant.

The attendant cleared her throat, trying to get the attention of the gate agent standing behind the counter. The agent ignored her and continued to peck at the computer with a line of customers in front of her.

"Stay here," the flight attendant ordered.

The boys watched as she went across the hall to monitors mounted on the wall. She stood still for a moment as she read the flight arrival information.

"Sorry, guys," she said when she came back. "I hate to be the bearer of bad news, but it's just like I expected—the flight from Memphis is *delayed*. The plane is in route now and won't be here until two o'clock. We started out there this morning—it was a stormy mess."

"*Two* o'clock!" they both shouted out.

"Our contest starts then. We *can't* wait," Max informed her.

"I'm afraid you're going to *have* to wait," the lady said. "I'll tell the gate agent to watch over you until your aunt arrives."

The boys looked gloomily at her, like she had just told them the worst news in the world. They followed her to an area behind the gate agent that was well hidden by a partition wall, so at least they didn't have to withstand gaping stares from customers in line at the podium.

The seats in this section were against the divider wall and faced a huge window that overlooked the tarmac. The boys could see a long caravan of carts behind a motorized vehicle delivering luggage to the plane parked at the jetway in front of them. The men worked furiously lifting the luggage off of the carts and loading it into the cargo department underneath the plane's cabin. Their mom had told them that this stowage area is also called the plane's belly.

Sam chuckled. He now knew why it's called this—the workers looked like they were feeding the oversized plane all sorts of stuff: suitcases, boxes, strollers, wheel-chairs, and even cages with pets in them.

"How could you laugh at a time like this?" Max grumbled to him. "We're going to miss the Knights of Knowledge contest. Maybe you don't care, but I worked for *days* on the thing."

Sam sighed, remembering. It was a shame they had to miss the contest because of weather in a city hundreds of miles from them. In New York, it was sunny and beautiful outside—the *perfect* weather to travel about the city.

"I don't think we should let the weather in Memphis stop us," Sam blurted out. "Surely Mom would agree that it would be tragic to let your hard work go to waste."

"Oh brother," Max said, staring at Sam intently. "What are you thinking?"

Sam didn't answer him. He stood up instead and nervously peeked his head around the wall to spy on the gate agent.

She was busier than ever. The flight display sign above her head read, "flight delayed due to a mechanical," and the line in front of her was full of angry people. Sam heard a man at the counter demanding to be rebooked, saying he was going to miss an important wedding if the plane didn't leave right away.

The agent scratched her head, looking as though she wished she could disappear behind the partition, too. She politely responded back to the man, who was now red in the face and was shouting for his wife to get his blood pressure medicine.

"I'm sorry about this, sir," the agent said sympathetically. "But it's simply out of my control. I'm sure you wouldn't want to fly on a plane that's not fixed. That wouldn't be safe for you or our other passengers."

She paused and then worked feverishly, typing things into her computer. "No," she confirmed after a couple of minutes. "There are no flights that would get to Atlanta any sooner. Please be patient and take a seat."

The agent stood her ground, looking the man squarely in the eyes, but Sam could see her leg nervously twitch behind the counter. She sighed with relief when the man moved toward his wife, who was coaxing him over with pills in her hand.

"Come take your medicine, dear," she called out to him. "Getting upset is not good for your health."

When the hot-headed man had stumbled off, the agent put on a brave front and shouted, "Next."

Sam had seen enough. He turned around to his brother and smiled, giving him the thumbs-up sign.

With this signal, Max gently placed his bag over his shoulder and quietly sneaked off, hiding behind the huge crowd that had congregated around the podium. He removed the conspicuous sticker from his shirt, and Sam quickly followed his lead.

The boys sped down the hallway and didn't slow down for anything—not electric carts beeping in the corridor or slow walkers—until they had sprinted down another long corridor, past security, and down the escalator to the baggage claim area.

Once they arrived there, they could see their bags, the last ones left, still moving in a circle on the belt. A man in a uniform was moving toward their luggage.

Max and Sam arrived in the nick of time to claim them. "Those are ours, sir," Max said, gasping for breath. "We got held up."

The man looked curiously at them for a moment before hurrying off to work another flight. The boys grabbed their bags off of the carousel and sprinted out the door toward the taxis.

It was a madhouse in this area. Angry

adults were fighting over cabs—throwing tantrums—pushing and shoving their way to the front of the long transportation line.

The drivers weren't any more civil or mature. They acted like little kids, too—squealing their tires as they peeled out and lying on their horns if another cab got in their way. It looked like a circus for obnoxious people with no ringmaster in sight.

One driver shouted to a timid old woman, "Hey lady, hop in. What are you waiting for? You think I've got all day?"

Max and Sam looked at each other wide-eyed, wondering what they had gotten themselves into. Then a yellow and black cab drove up and an older man with wild, frizzy gray hair got out of his vehicle. He took pity on them.

"Do you boys need a ride?" he yelled.

"Um, yes, I guess so," Max stammered.

"Come on, before you get eaten alive," he called out to them.

The driver walked to the back of his cab as Max and Sam rolled their suitcases toward him. They must have looked frightened out of their minds because he said, "Don't worry. I just *look* crazy, but I'm not really." He laughed and said, "My name is Charlie. Why are a couple of youngsters like you traveling alone in such a big place like New York?"

"We need to go to the Great Lawn in Central Park," Max blurted out, ignoring the question.

"Do you have thirty bucks for the cab fare?" the driver asked.

Max reached into his pocket to find the money his mom had given him to buy souvenirs. Relieved, he felt the crisp paper of the bills brush against his fingertips.

"We have the money," Max said.

"We're in business then," the man said, pleased. "I'll get you to the park by one o'clock."

FOUR

GHARLIE THE CABDRIVER

If Max and Sam thought the airport was a zoo, traveling on the streets of New York was even worse. . . . It was gut-wrenching and brutal.

The boys dug their fingers into the back of the seat in front of them and tried to keep from yelling out as Charlie mercilessly went in and out of cars like he was on a race to Central Park—a race with *whom* they didn't know. At one point, he even drove onto the grass at the side of the street to get around a car that he shouted was as slow as molasses.

"Geez Louise!" he cried out, trying to adjust his usual vocabulary. Every so often, a bad curse word would slip out and he would apologize profusely.

"Don't worry," he would yell, as he slung the car this way and that. "I've been driving a cab for thirty years. I'm a profes-sional."

"Yikes," Sam responded, in a shrill voice that made him sound like he was on a run-a-way train.

"Can you slow down?" Max finally yelled out, when he didn't think he could take it anymore. "I don't want to die."

"*Die?*" Charlie said, laughing hysteri-cally. "I've been at this for years—and have only ten wrecks on my record."

"*Ten?*" Sam shrieked. "Did anyone *die* in them?"

"Just one poor old man," Charlie said

somberly. He waited a few seconds and then burst out laughing. "Just kidding. He didn't *die*—he just got hurt. Besides, the wreck wasn't *really* my fault, only the incompetent insurance company said so."

The conviction in Charlie's voice and the confidence he displayed persuaded the boys that the driver really *believed* what he was saying was true.

"Thank goodness you have a seasoned driver in your presence," Charlie bragged. "These roads are not for the weak. I was born and raised on these streets."

"Did you get the scar on your face from one of the accidents?" Max asked timidly.

"As a matter of fact, I did," Charlie answered, more proud than ever. "It makes me look tough. Don't you think?"

Charlie suddenly switched lanes and darted around the right side of a car, ignoring the rule about only passing on the left. The cab almost hit the side of a bridge, jerking onto the road at the last second.

Max and Sam were too scared to scream. They held their breath, instead, and remained speechless while Charlie traveled through noisy streets and then finally pulled up across the street from a gigantic stone building. The sign that hung down from this eye-catching structure read, "American Museum of Natural History." To their right was a large tree-filled area that seemed out of place in the building-packed city.

"Is that Central Park?" Sam blurted out, feeling safe and comforted already.

"Yep, New York's pride and joy," the driver beamed. "There's not a New Yorker that wouldn't give his left eye for this park. It's a place where people from all parts of the city come together to have picnics, listen to a concert, or walk their dogs. Without this park, New York would be a congested city, full of steel, high-rise buildings and uptight people. This is the place that calms all of our souls." He smiled fondly and then pointed. "That trail will lead you to the Great Lawn," he said.

"Thanks. This place sounds pretty special," Max said, reaching in his pocket and handing Charlie the money for the fare.

After the boys had gotten out and traveled down the winding trail for a few minutes, Sam noticed a large field of grass across the way and a man dressed like a knight standing by a booth. He wore an elaborate costume and a fake mustache and beard. One part of his mustache kept coming unstuck and drooping down into his mouth, finally making him mad enough to tear the patch of hair off and toss it into a nearby trash can. A fancy wooden easel beside him held a sign that read, "Knights of Knowledge contest." Below that, it read, "May wisdom be your guide."

Sam then noticed a gallant knight on a horse. He found it fascinating to see a medieval soldier in the middle of a modern city like New York. As the sun shone down upon the knight, rays of light bounced off his armor. The horse's shiny coat glistened in the soft sunlight.

BELVEDERE CASTLE

Max and Sam were thrilled they had made it to Central Park in one piece, even with an hour to spare. As they waited in the long line to check in for the contest, they looked around at the buzz of activity.

A man with a guitar sang softly in front of a small audience. . . . A horse pulling an old-fashioned carriage galloped by. . . . An elderly couple holding hands walked along, occasionally stopping to watch children play. . . . An old man in shabby shoes whistled as he danced to music. . . . This park *was* magical. The greenery melted stress away—from the old, young, rich, and poor alike.

They finally made it to the front of the check-in line. "Your names please," the attendant said, interrupting their kaleidoscope of imagery.

"Max and Sam Stone," Max answered, his voice quivering. "Do you have a place we can stow our suitcases?"

The man didn't seem to notice Max's nervousness, instead he scoured over the list in front of him. "Oh, yes, there are your names. Your registration fee has been paid in full. You can stow your luggage in the tent over there, but be sure to pick it up before ten. I take it that you have money for the subway." He looked up from the rim of his glasses and waited for a reply.

Max nodded.

"Excellent," the man said, handing them

a small wooden knight painted with gold paint. "Present the knight at each station to get your next riddle. The contest will begin at the entrance to Belvedere Castle, across the pond," he said, pointing. "Follow the trail to get there. We've lit the street lamps to lead the way to this magnificent castle," the man said proudly. "Contest will begin at two o'clock sharp."

Max and Sam stared across the pond at the gray-rock structure, its towers rising

high above the trees. An American flag ruffled in the wind above one of its turrets.

The boys thanked the contest clerk and went to the tent to stow their suitcases. After that, they skirted off with their small bags over their shoulders, not wanting to draw attention to the fact they were alone.

As they followed the flaming torches around the meandering path, they looked at giant elms and pink-blossomed trees that were scattered about. Other paths curled off in different directions.

As they walked, Max explained that the old stone castle was built in 1869 as a decorative shell of windows and doors and was taken over by the U.S. Weather Bureau in 1912. "It is now a visitor center, but temperature readings for the park are still taken from there," he said. "*Belvedere* means beautiful view in Italian."

"What else is in this park?" Sam asked. "I thought that parks only had hiking trails and trees in them."

"Not *this* park," Max said. "It has a lot of things besides walking trails . . . children's playgrounds . . . an outdoor theater . . . a zoo . . . and ice-skating rinks for the winter. The Great Lawn, where we checked in, is used for many things."

"Why do they call it the Great Lawn?" Sam asked curiously.

"Maybe because it's large," Max said, shrugging his shoulders. "I read that it's fifty-five acres in size. People play sports on it, have concerts there, and who knows what else. It once was a reservoir until it was filled in with dirt to create a lawn."

The boys continued to follow the pathway. Metal knight statues were placed alongside it to add ambience to the medieval theme. The boys trudged up a steep hill and then up stone steps to reach the castle entrance area. A group of people holding little gold knights surrounded a man in a knight suit. A rectangular terrace looked out over the surrounding area and offered a fantastic view of an outdoor theater, large pond, and the Great Lawn.

"Thirty more minutes," the gentleman called out in a gruff voice.

Max and Sam looked around at the fifty or so people that packed the area. One man wore metal-rimmed glasses like the booth clerk and looked much like a college professor. One lady was decked to the hills in a frilly dress, feathered hat, and high heels, looking more like she was going to a party than a contest. How would she get around the city dressed like *that*? There were some children in the crowd, but not many.

"What were we thinking when we entered this contest?" Sam said. "Most of these people look so old and wise."

"Don't worry," Max said, grinning. "They probably think we look young and clever."

Six

SUBWAY STATION

T he knight's voice boomed through the chattering crowd. "ATTENTION!"

The contestants jerked their faces toward the powerful voice.

"The contest is ready to begin," he bellowed out. "When I say on your mark—get set—go, climb the inside stairs to the second-floor terrace of the castle, where you will find rolls of paper in a basket. Take one and read the first riddle, which will lead you to your next destination."

The knight took a deep breath and shouted with all his might, "On your mark—get set—GO!"

As the crowd thundered by, the brothers shrunk together for fear of getting trampled, like ants on a playground. After the last person had stormed past them, they made their way inside the castle.

As the boys entered, many people brushed against them on their way out the door. They saw the professor, coming down the narrow steps leading to the second floor, with a basket in his arms. He handed a roll to Max as well as other contestants left in the small reception area.

Max suddenly sensed he was being watched. He slowly looked around at the crowd and caught the eye of a red-haired woman, who was in a room off of the entrance area. She quickly glanced away.

Max untied a gold ribbon and unrolled beige paper. He read the clues out loud.

This was a gift from France and a symbol of freedom as well.

It's as famous as Philadelphia's Liberty Bell.

"I know this one," Sam said. "The rhyme is about the Statue of Liberty. But where is it?"

Max found the right page in his book, and they both read silently:

The Statue of Liberty, officially titled Liberty Enlightening the World, is a universal symbol of democracy. It was given to the USA as a present from France to celebrate America's one-hundredth birthday. It arrived on June 17, 1885, onboard the French ship *Isère,* in 350 copper pieces housed in 214 crates. Amazingly, the ship almost sank in rough seas during the voyage. The statue wasn't assembled until its concrete and granite base was completed, more than a year later. On October 28, 1886, the pieces were assembled, facing southeast toward the Atlantic, for the world to see.

The statue stands 305 feet tall from the ground to the tip of its flare, the height of a twenty-two-story building. Its torch symbolizes lighting the way to freedom, and its seven rays on its crown represent the seven seas and seven continents. Its tablet is inscribed in Roman numerals, July 4, 1776, the date of America's independence. In 1986, the original torch was replaced with one bearing a flame plated in twenty-four-karat gold. The old torch is displayed inside the entrance lobby of the statue. Over the years, the process of patination, or the oxidation of the copper, caused the statue to turn green. The thick green coat protects the statue's copper from deteriorating. Because of the conductive nature of copper, the statue is struck by

lightning several times a year.
To get to the statue: Take the subway to Battery Park and catch the ferry that goes to Liberty Island.

Max and Sam followed the professor out of the castle and down stairs beside the terrace. He led them down a path that ended at a street. The boys were just about to ask him for directions to the subway when they heard a loud *honk-honk*. They turned their heads to see Charlie, sticking his head out of his cab window. "I thought I recognized you two. Can I give you a free lift?" he said, grinning. "It's the least I can do after scaring you to death. I promise to drive slowly—scout's honor."

The boys looked at each other, trying to decide if they should trust him again.

"Okay," Max said, as he and Sam slid into the backseat. "We need to go to a subway stop to catch a train to Battery Park."

The New Yorker knew just where to go.

He drove down the street and turned around, heading back up the same street, so that he could drive along the park's perimeter and point out famous park sites. "There's Strawberry Fields," he said, nodding to his left. "It was named after a song by the Beatles to honor John Lennon. Sadly, he lived and died near here."

After a few minutes, he made another turn and said, "The park zoo is close by. I hope you don't mind my taking the long way around so you can see some of the things in the south part of the park."

The boys were worried about the time, but they didn't want to rush the cabdriver for fear he'd drive like a maniac again. Amazingly, right now Charlie was relaxed, almost like he was going on a tour himself.

After a few minutes, they came to a plaza. The boys could see the carriage horse they had seen earlier in the park. It was standing patiently behind another car-

riage, waiting for its next patron.

Charlie drove by the plaza and down a couple of streets before finally pulling over. "The subway stop is just down those stairs," he said, staring at a street corner.

As soon as they thanked him and got out, they could hear the rumbling of trains underneath. They went down the stairs to a dim underground station. They pinched their noses to escape from an odd smell.

"It's spooky down here," Max said, inching toward a nicely dressed woman in a pantsuit. "Ma'am, can you tell us which train to get on to go to Battery Park?"

She smiled. "You must be planning to catch the ferry to the Statue of Liberty," she said. "I work on Wall Street. Your stop will be right after mine. Can you believe my boss is making me do paperwork on a holiday? I slipped away for a while and went shopping just to spite him." She suddenly giggled like a naughty schoolgirl.

She helped the boys purchase subway tickets from a machine, and then they followed the lady through an automated turnstile and down more stairs to a platform. Both of the boys covered their ears at the horrific sound of a train screeching to a halt in front of them. A door opened, and they followed the lady onto a silver train.

SEVEN

THE ISLANDS

Max and Sam enjoyed the cool, gentle breeze as they sat on the top level of the ferry as it made its way to Liberty Island. Sam smiled smugly, still surprised his plan to move to the front of the long boarding line at Battery Park had worked. He had simply told the boarding agent that they were part of a contest, showing him their knight as proof—and *voilà*—they were able to board first, ahead of others.

As the large ferry boat rocked softly from side to side as it traveled through the choppy water, Max turned to Sam. "Did you know that in 1986, on the statue's hundredth birthday, the largest firework display in this country's history was set off?"

Sam's eyes lit up, thinking about red, white, and blue sparks bursting in the sky.

As the ferry boat passed the front of the statue, the boys could see the robed figure

off to their side, holding a torch up in the air, looking even more spectacular than they expected. The statue stood proud and solemn with broken shackles at its feet, as if it knew what an important icon it had become. Having to go to an island to visit the statue, made it all the more special.

"I can see why so many people from all over the world want to come to America now," Sam said, gazing at the patriotic site. "We have so much freedom here."

When the ferry had docked to the side of the statue, Max and Sam followed the crowd down a long paved walkway. At the end, they found a circular area at the edge of the island where an American flag flapped about in the wind. Gray and white birds circled around this area, and Manhattan, the island in New York they had just come from, could be seen in the backdrop across the rippling water. A man dressed like a knight stood by the flagpole.

When they went over to him, the knight did not respond. "Clue please," Max said.

The man remained silent.

When Sam took the wooden knight from his pocket and handed it to him, the knight came alive and nodded. He wrote an "S" on the back in dark ink and gave them another riddle that read:

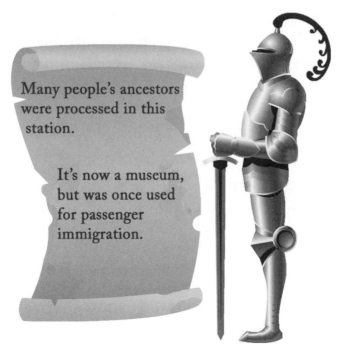

Many people's ancestors were processed in this station.

It's now a museum, but was once used for passenger immigration.

"Off to the next stop," the knight commanded.

The boys jumped at the sound of his boisterous voice and stumbled away, only stopping a safe distance away.

"The riddle is talking about Ellis Island. The ferry operator said the boat stops there on the way back to the city," Max said.

Max thumbed through his book until he reached the part about the historic island. It read:

Ellis Island served as a federal immigration station from 1892 until 1954, processing over twelve million ship passengers. It is estimated that forty percent of Americans have an ancestor who entered the country through this station. In 1965, the island was declared to be part of the Statue of Liberty National Monument. In 1990, it became an immigration museum.

Max and Sam sprinted back to the dock

and followed a trail of people onto the boat just before its boarding doors were closed.

The curious boys scurried over to the side of the boat to look through a long window and watch workers untie the ropes that had anchored the ferry to the dock.

They saw grave disappointment on the faces of a group standing on the gangplank who had just missed the boat. Max and Sam recognized them as some of the contestants from the park.

After a short ride in the water, the boys were starting to feel seasick and were relieved when the ferry's captain announced, "We will now be docking at Ellis Island. Its museum offers a fascinating look at American immigration. Many of you have ancestors who passed through this station and don't even realize it."

"I wish we had time to tour the museum," Sam said. "It sounds interesting."

"I wish," Max said, walking down the

ramp of the ferry boat, "but we can't risk falling behind."

"Look," Sam said, pointing to a passenger behind them. "Is that the red-haired lady from the park?"

Max turned around to check, but a tall stocky man blocked his view. He could only see a glimpse of red hair.

Sam's eyes suddenly flared with excitement. "There's a knight!" he said, looking toward the island.

This friendly knight was a stark contrast to the last one. He was by a tree, smiling and waving to the arriving passengers, welcoming them with open arms.

When Max and Sam greeted him and handed him their knight, he got even chummier. "Congratulations!" he said, slapping their backs and making them cough. "You're my first visitors. Any more contestants on the boat?"

"Maybe a red-haired lady we first saw

at Central Park," Sam replied.

"If you want to stay in first place, you better keep moving," he teased. "Here's your riddle. I've marked your knight. Only four stops to finish."

"*Four*?" Max mumbled out loud.

Sam unrolled the riddle that read:

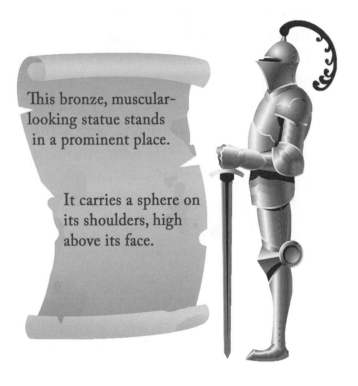

This bronze, muscular-looking statue stands in a prominent place.

It carries a sphere on its shoulders, high above its face.

"I've seen a picture of that statue in the book," Max said, rummaging through his bag to find the handy guide.

Max and Sam huddled around the book as Max turned its pages. He found the photo of the statue on a page about Rockefeller Center. The paragraph underneath the photo said:

This forty-five-foot bronze sculpture and base, the Statue of Atlas, portrays a bulky and strong Atlas holding up a sphere with rings. Across the statue's shoulders is a wide beam that displays symbols representing the planets. In mythology, Atlas was the titan who held up the heavens. This statue is the largest sculpture in Rockefeller Center, a complex located in Midtown New York that has nineteen buildings spread across twenty-two acres. This massive center includes offices, gardens, and even a rink for ice skating.

"Let's get back on the ferry!" Sam said.

They scampered back to the water and boarded the ferry in the nick of time. As they stood by the railing and looked out at the water, the boat slowly made its way back to the city. As the boat cruised along in the harbor, the air smelled fresh, and the breeze ruffled their shirts.

A short time later, the boys raced down the bridgeway and onto land. As they scurried through the shady park, they passed the old fort, Clinton Castle, where they had purchased ferry tickets. Then they raced past an American flag before crossing a street and pausing in front of an elaborate building called U.S. Custom House. Its tall stone columns and statues perched on top made this monument regal and grand.

Suddenly, Max stopped dead in his tracks. . . . He slowly looked behind them. He looked to the side of them. Why did he keep getting the sense that they were being followed?

THE GOOD DEED

Max and Sam's mouths watered as they stood outside a deli down from the subway station whose sign proclaimed it sold the best reuben sandwiches in the city. They hadn't eaten since breakfast-- if you dare to count the pea-size muffin from the plane a meal, that is. As they gazed at the sandwich display in the deli's window, they drooled dreamily at the layers of thinly sliced juicy meat stacked between two pieces of homemade bread.

It was in the middle of this scrumptious

fantasy when Sam thought he heard a groan. He looked farther down the sidewalk and discovered a lady shaking violently, doubled over in distress.

He ran over to her. "Are you okay?" he said, frightened.

"No," she heaved out. "I need some juice." She began to shake even more.

"I'll be right back," he assured her.

Sam shouted for Max to call 911 to get an ambulance as he ran down the sidewalk and through the deli door. "Use the cell phone Mom gave us," he reminded him.

Inside the deli, there was no one in sight. "Help, someone!" Sam pleaded loudly. "There's a sick lady outside."

A man came from the kitchen with a soiled apron on and a knife still in his hand. In an instant, the man had retrieved a bottle of juice from a refrigerator behind the counter and had handed it to him.

When Sam darted out the door and returned to the lady, he was horrified to find her lying on the ground, still shaking and unable to talk. He opened the cap and held the bottle up to her mouth, tilting it so that a stream could flow into her trembling mouth. The lady swallowed the sweet liquid as if her life depended on it, and after a few mouthfuls, she recovered enough to sit up and hold the bottle herself.

A vehicle with a blaring siren noisily weaved in and out of traffic until it pulled up to the curb beside them. Its siren shut off, and two men dressed in white jackets jumped out and ran over, asking the lady questions and examining her with instruments. They left for a moment and came back with a stretcher, gently placing her on the canvas cot.

The loud vehicle had caused a stir and curious onlookers gathered around. One of the paramedics tipped his hat toward the boys as if to say good job.

The lady smiled warmly at Sam, her eyes twinkling with gratitude. "Thank you," she said softly. "If it wasn't for you, I'd be in a diabetic coma by now." She thanked both of them again and again as the men carried her away on the stretcher.

Sam's stomach growled, and he realized he was hungrier than ever. The thought of delicious food made him turn and race for the deli door. Max followed close behind him. Just as they walked in, the siren began to roar again in the background.

"Looks like she's going to be okay," the deli owner said, watching through the window as the ambulance zigzagged its way down the busy street bound for the hospital. "It's amazing how many people don't take the time to help these days. Order anything you like. It's on the house."

Did he say order *anything*? His words were music to their tired ears.

THE ALLEY

It felt wonderful to be walking toward Rockefeller Center with full stomachs. The boys were convinced that New York had the best delis in the world.

As they strolled along, they watched people hustle in and out of fashionable shops and disappear into brick, brass-numbered apartment buildings. The boys were starting to like the excitement of being in a city that was alive with activity.

Sam noticed a Statue of Liberty replica on display in a dress shop window and stopped to admire it, wishing he had enough money to buy it. A lady in a pink linen suit cheerfully waved to him from inside. Sam waved back and then noticed his brother a few feet away. He was acting oddly, peeking into an alley and crouching by the store wall.

"Shhh," he whispered when Sam got near him. "Stay back."

Sam got on his knees and peeked into the alley, spying two men loading paintings into the back of a beat-up van.

The boys heard one of the men say, "Hurry up. The owner will be back soon. Did you get the Van Gogh?"

A light-haired man with fair, freckled skin shot back at him. "Of course, I did. What do you think I am, a *dunce*?"

"Maybe I do," the other man yelled. "After you messed up the last job so bad."

"Something tells me they're not talking about a job as we know it," Sam whispered into Max's ear. "What should we do?"

Max stepped back on the sidewalk and shuffled through his bag to find his camera. He nestled down low and got the men in his lens. He snapped several photos before his brother pulled him away.

"I've got an idea," Sam said, whispering. "Let's go in the shop and snap a photo of the van's license plate through the window. The alley is so narrow that the van will have to come this way to get out."

"Good idea," Max whispered back, happy at the thought of being inside.

"Do you want to purchase the Statue of Liberty in the window?" the woman said when they walked in. She smiled and then tried to entice Sam. "It's on sale today."

"Can we look around?" he asked.

"Look around as long as you want," she said cordially. "I'll be in the back if you need any help."

Max and Sam waited anxiously until she

disappeared from sight and then ran over to the corner to squat beside the side window. They stayed low to the ground so they wouldn't be detected. Max got the camera ready, worried that his battery would die before the van drove by.

Finally, after several minutes, the green van came into view, stopping at the end of the alley.

The angle of the shot couldn't have been

more perfect. . . . The window wrapped around from the front to the side, enabling Max to position himself to get a bird's eye view of the license plate. He shot as many photos as he could before the van turned right onto the street.

The boys ran to the back of the store.

"Miss, oh miss," Sam called out.

It was only seconds before she came out of the inventory room, smiling pleasantly.

"Sorry to interrupt you," Sam started out by saying.

"We need to report a crime," Max said, getting to the business at hand. "We shot photos of two men in a van loading up stolen paintings in the alley by this store. We took photos of their license plate, too. Will you call the police and give them our camera as evidence?"

The lady stared blankly at them for a moment and then reality set in. "*What?* *Where?*" she shrieked, running in circles.

Max and Sam watched in disbelief, shocked at how a composed lady had turned into a raving lunatic before their eyes. She continued her frenzy until Sam gently took hold of her arms.

"Calm down," he said slowly, looking into her eyes. "The thieves are long gone. We've got to go now. We're in the middle of a contest."

The lady blushed with embarrassment as she tried to pull herself together. "And what contest is that, dear?" she said, straightening the collar of her suit.

"The Knights of Knowledge contest," Max said proudly.

"Don't worry," the lady said, looking in a compact mirror to put her hair back in place. "I've got it under control. What shall I tell the police your names are?"

"Max and Sam Stone," one of the boys called out to her as they sprinted through the shop and out the door.

Times Square

*A*s the boys walked down a long street lined with buildings with American flags on them, their eyes were transfixed on a stunning gothic cathedral that stood in the middle of modern buildings. Its elaborate towers looked like thin stone mountains. A lady in the subway told them that the giant statue was across the street from this church.

"Did you know that Rockefeller Center has almost five hundred elevators and the largest theater in the *world*?" Max quizzed his brother while they walked.

"This is a pretty spectacular place," Sam said, looking around at the impressive buildings that were so elegant and stately.

Within minutes, the boys found the towering bronze sculpture just where the lady informed them it would be.

"Greetings," a well-groomed knight said as they approached the statue. "May I see your knight please?"

The man carefully wrote an "A" on the back, using his best handwriting. "Enjoy the view of the magnificent Atlas Statue," he said enthusiastically, handing them a rolled-up piece of paper. "Good evening, fine lads." He bowed before them.

"He sure does take his job seriously," Sam whispered into Max's ear.

The boys gawked at the colossal metal masterpiece one last time before moving away from the attentive knight. They huddled together to read the next riddle.

It's a place where thousands of people gather for a ball to drop to signal the start of a new year.

Broadway shows and huge digital signs are here.

"The riddle is talking about Times Square," Sam said excitedly. "That's where the ball drops on New Year's Eve."

"I think I read in the book that Times Square is near here," Max said.

"Miss," Sam said, stopping a woman on the street. "Can you tell us where the ball drops on New Year's Eve?"

"Yeah, it's a few streets over," she said, motioning with her hand.

The boys listened intently as she gave them directions, and then they hurried down the crowded street. They spotted a man in a gold-striped uniform and hat standing in front of a building with a green awning and shiny brass doors. The gentleman took great care to greet each person coming inside the building, opening the door and welcoming him or her home.

"That's a doorman," Max informed his brother. "Fancy places have them."

Sam grinned, thinking that he could get used to the lifestyle that a city offered.

After several more minutes, the boys had reached Times Square. This section of town was as chaotic and hectic as it looked on television. Enormous lit-up advertisements flashed from screens in all directions. Hordes of people passed by, some making their way into shops and restaurants and some making their way to a Broadway show. Max and Sam felt a surge of energy just being there.

It wasn't long before they spotted a hip young knight standing in front of a police station, below a tower of illuminated signs where two streets came together.

The boys struggled to cross the lane of busy traffic and finally reached him.

"What's up, dudes?" he said with his hands loose to his side. "How's this contest treating ya?" He paused to look at their faces and then suddenly developed an attitude. "It must not be treating ya that well because—*dudes*—I hate to break this to ya—but you're in *last* place. Why don't ya give up and catch a Broadway show?"

"Aren't you supposed to be *encouraging* us?" Sam snapped at him.

"No offense, but this is just a day job to get me through the summer until college starts back," he said casually.

"We're *not* quitting," Max said.

"Well, good luck then," he said, writing a "T" on the back of their knight. "Yer gonna need it. Here's some hints for ya."

Max unrolled the paper and read the clues about their next destination:

This museum is called MOMA to abbreviate its name.

It houses modern works of arts by artists who have achieved great fame.

The Last Clue

The last riddle had been easy to solve since their dad had visited the Museum of Modern Art before. Ironically, their dad had given them a brochure from the museum and Max had been using it as a bookmark in their city guide.

The boys could see why their dad had liked the place so much. From what they saw from the lobby, it showcased lively, interesting art—*so* abstract, in fact, that you couldn't tell what most of the objects in the paintings even were.

"I guess that's why they call the art *modern*," Sam surmised, as they walked toward the next landmark.

Max still had the riddle in his pocket that they had gotten from the knight at the museum. It read:

This skyscraper is the tallest building in the city and has a pinnacle that points up in the air.

It has offices and two observation decks built with an art-deco flair.

By this time, Manhattan was busier than ever. Drivers honked their horns in the jammed traffic as a flood of people filled the sidewalk—dashing into markets, dry cleaners, and lofty buildings.

"So this is what the city is like at night," Sam said, shaking his head at the madness.

"The Empire State Building should be our last stop," Max said. "The knight at Ellis Island said we had four stops to go, and this is the fourth."

"Oh yeah, he did say that," Sam said.

Max stopped to get his book out of his bag. He thumbed through the guide to get to the information about the soaring skyscraper. As they walked, he read out loud:

The Empire State Building, the first structure to have over a hundred floors, was completed in 1931 and stood as the world's tallest building for more than forty years, until the completion of the World Trade Center's North Tower in 1972. After the September 11, 2001 attacks on the twin towers of the World Trade Center, the Empire State Building once again became the tallest in New York; however, over the years, there have been several buildings constructed in the world that are taller. The Empire State Building has 102 floors and stands 1454 feet to the top of its lightning rod, making it the second tallest building in America. Its rod gets struck by lightning about a hundred times a year. It offers a great view of the city from its eighty-sixth-floor outdoor observation deck and features a theatrical presentation on its second floor in which passengers are seated in a motion simulator that takes you on an aerial tour of the city.

"The simulator ride sounds pretty cool," Sam said, ushering Max over to the side to keep him from getting run over by a bicycle. "Since this is the last stop, maybe we can go on it. It would be nice to sit down and rest our feet."

As they walked toward the Empire State Building, letting its trademark pinnacle be their guide, suspicious people began to pop out of the woodwork. . . . A scruffy man wearing tattered clothing eyed them as they walked by. . . . Another man with a matted beard laughed eerily as they crept by him. It seemed like the closer to dark it got, the more frightening the city became.

The prominent skyscraper was easy to spot as it towered over the other buildings with its contemporary design. As they stood in front of it, they were confused because a knight wasn't anywhere in sight.

Max recognized one of the contestants walking out of the building, holding a ribbon in his hand and grinning widely.

"There's the professor-looking man with the glasses," Max said. "It looks like he may have won the contest."

"At least a good guy finished first," Sam said, looking on the bright side. "It was pretty nice of him to bring the basket down to hand out the rolls of paper."

"Can you tell us where the knight is?" Max said, approaching him.

"Inside," he said. "Hey, are you the boys who took photos of the art thieves?"

"Y-y-y-yeah," Max stammered, "How did you know *that*?"

"They're waiting for you," the man said with a mischievous grin.

Max looked down. "I think we're a little late for a prize," he responded back.

Once the boys had made their way through the revolving doors of the famous building, they went down a narrow hallway and then spotted a man in a knight suit standing in front of an escalator. They ran over to him and wearily handed him their wooden knight.

"Glad you guys made it," he said with a crooked smile, almost as if he had been waiting specifically for them. He wrote an "E" on the back and handed them another roll of paper.

"I thought this is our last stop," Sam said, confused.

"You're right," he said with a gleam in his eye. "It most certainly is."

Max and Sam couldn't help but think that people were acting strangely—first the professor and now this knight.

Max shrugged it off and untied what he hoped would be the last riddle. He read:

Look at the letters that have been written on the back of your knight.

Examine them closely and let knowledge be your guiding light.

Sam turned over the wooden knight, and they focused on its hand-written letters:

S E A T M E

After a minute, Sam broke the silence. "Look!" he yelled. "The words 'seat me' are spelled out! What does that mean?"

Max wrinkled his brow and concentrated on all that he had learned.

"It must have something to do with this building since it's the last stop," Sam said.

"I know," Max blurted out. "The theater ride. It's called the New York Skyride."

"That's it!" Sam agreed, nodding his head in certainty. "The book said that passengers are *seated* for a simulator ride."

"The theater room is on the second floor, right?" Sam asked the knight.

The knight winked to confirm it.

The boys dashed up the escalator and were directed to a security checkpoint.

OLD MYSTERIES

The weary brothers finally made it through security and turned a corner. Suddenly, a storm of applause erupted, a noise so loud it made the boys jump. They looked around in confusion.

Max and Sam's heads spun, trying to figure out what was going on. They were puzzled because they knew the professor and probably many others had gotten there before them to claim the prizes.

The red-haired lady whom they had seen at the castle in the park and outside the ferry moved toward them. She looked like she was about to burst from excitement. A little girl about their age stood to her side.

"Hello, boys," she said, squealing with delight. "I've been waiting for years to see you." She draped her arms around them and held them close for several seconds.

The boys were motionless.

"I'm your Aunt Janice, and I'm sure you recognize your cousin Madison," she said, breaking free. "Excuse my manners, but I couldn't resist hugging you. I haven't laid eyes on you since you were toddlers."

"Uh—uh," is all that Sam could get out.

"How did you find us?" Max said.

"We arrived at the park just as you were checking in," she said. "I'm surprised you didn't catch Madison hiding behind that knight by the path, watching you."

"Your flight wasn't supposed to get in until two," Max said, stunned.

"We took a flight on another airline and

arrived just as the airport staff was in panic mode, trying to find you," their aunt said. "You guys caused quite a stir." She laughed wickedly. "It would be just the sort of trouble I would have gotten into as a kid. I had a feeling you went on to the park since your luggage had been picked up, so Madison and I flagged a cab and skedaddled right down there, arriving around one-thirty."

"Why didn't you tell us you were there?" Max asked, puzzled.

"I wanted to at first," she said. "But Madison convinced me that it would be more fun for you guys to compete alone— under my watchful, hidden eye, of course."

"If you were following us, how did you get here *before* us?" Sam said, confused.

"While you were talking to the man with the glasses, we slipped inside the building and followed another contestant to the second floor," their aunt explained.

Max looked around at the crowd. "Did we win third place or something?"

"Heavens no," Aunt Janice laughed giddily. "You actually came in *last* place, but that's beside the point. There's more important things than winning like—"

Their aunt stopped to squeal with excitement again. "You boys, my nephews I'm proud to say, were going around the city being little heroes—saving a lady from going into a coma and snapping photos of art thieves along the way. Goodness, Madison and I didn't even know you did *that* until we got here—we wondered why you were in that shop for so long. Don't you know . . . these people want to give you a special award for your bravery."

The crowd erupted in applause again, cheering and whistling, as a man with an expensive-looking suit and polished shoes moved his way to the front.

The man held up his hands to silence the

group and then turned toward the boys. "It gives me great pleasure, as mayor of New York," he announced, "to give you both honorary keys to the city. You are fine examples to youngsters everywhere."

He beamed at them for several minutes before he, as well as the crowd, trailed out of sight. Max and Sam stared awkwardly at the big gold keys in their hands and then at their aunt until she spoke.

"Oh, I almost forgot. Did you like the map and old journal I sent you?" she said.

"*You* sent those?" Sam coughed out, almost choking on his words.

"Yeah . . . didn't you read the card?"

"NO!" the boys both yelled at once with their eyes bulging at her.

"Whoops," she said, realizing the impact of her negligence. "I must have forgotten to put the card in. Sometimes I'm so absent-minded, I reckon I'd forget to put my head on, if it wasn't already attached."

She informed them, "The journal was a prized possession of your late grandpa . . . and the map was one I drew myself in the fifth grade. I worked for days on that map," she recalled fondly. "So when I heard you were going on your first trip, I thought you might like to have the journal and map—seeing that you guys were going to be world travelers and all."

Max and Sam tried to absorb the shock.

"Did you know we've carried the journal on all of our trips?" Sam spoke finally, reaching in his bag to find it.

"Your grandpa would be so happy," she said, gleaming with pride.

"Aunt Janice, do you know about the letters on the map?" Max asked seriously.

"*Letters?*" she said. "Why yes, I wrote 'Max and Sam's Incredible Journey Map' at the top. I also wrote 'May good fortune be with you' at the bottom."

"Not *those* letters," Sam said, opening

up the journal and taking out the two pieces of the map. "*These* letters."

He pointed to the mysterious letters that had appeared on the map during their trips.

"Look!" he yelled out. "There's a new letter by the 'N.Y.' that dad had written before we left for New York."

Max, Sam, Aunt Janice, and their cousin Madison stared at an "M" that was undeniably there—written in bold black ink.

"We're sorry about the map tearing in two," Max said guiltily.

"That's okay," their aunt said, preoccupied. "Why don't you write the letters down on a page in the journal and figure out what they mean. My father always drilled into our heads, 'Notes taken wisely can be of great use to you.'"

"Our grandpa wrote the words on the first page of the journal!" Sam yelled out.

"Yes," their aunt said. "I'm sorry you didn't get to meet him. He was a smart

man. He lived by that motto, spending hours at a time, taking notes about the things he learned."

"Who wrote the date at the bottom of the map?" Max asked, remembering how it had been such a mystery to them.

"I did, when I drew the map," she said.

Sam wrote the letters, in the order they had appeared, on a page of the journal.

They all gaped at the letters:

W I S D O M

"Holy moly!" their aunt shouted out, flabbergasted. "It spells out the word 'wisdom' as clear as day."

Max, Sam, and Madison stood frozen and stared at the page in bewilderment.

"Oh, drat," Aunt Janice mumbled, looking at her watch. "We have to get to Central Park before ten to get our luggage. We better get moving."

"So what do you boys think about the subway?" she asked as they made their way down the escalator. "I didn't know what to think in the beginning. The train rattles so loudly as it races through those dark tunnels and then screeches to such a quick stop. I wanted to scream the first time we rode it. Madison held her hand over my mouth so I wouldn't alert you. We were just in the train car next to you."

Max and Sam smiled, realizing they had been watched over the entire time.

Sam suddenly turned to his aunt, panic-stricken. "Did the airline call Mom?"

"No, I spoke to them in time," she said, grimacing at the close call.

"Thanks," Max and Sam said, relieved.

As the four of them walked out of the tallest building in the city, darkness had set in, and fireworks exploded in the sky above them. It was the perfect ending to a day in the most fascinating city on earth.

MAX AND SAM'S SCIENCE PICK
Green Copper Pennies

Why is the Statue of Liberty green?

This experiment will reveal the answer since the Statue of Liberty is also made of copper.

Supplies needed: bowl, plate, paper towels, four pennies, and vinegar

Instructions:
1. Pour vinegar in a bowl and place the pennies in it.
2. Wad up a few paper towels and dip them in the vinegar.
3. Line the plate with the paper towels, placing the wet side on top.
4. Place the pennies on top of the vinegar-soaked paper towels and let them sit for a few hours. When you check on them, the top of the pennies will be green but the bottom will not.

Explanation: Vinegar, whose chemical name is acetic acid, combines with the copper to form a green coating that is composed of copper acetate. Oxygen must be present for this chemical reaction to occur. That is why the air-exposed sides of the pennies will be green and the other sides will remain a copper color. The acid in rainwater reacts with the Statue of Liberty's copper in the same way, causing it to turn green.